To:

From:

How to Catch a CLASS PET

From the
New York Times
Bestselling Series by
Alice Walstead &
Andy Elkerton

sourcebooks
wonderland

Summer was great, and we had so much fun!
There was biking, camp, and the pool!
Now we all have a new place to go—
together, we're all off to school!

Playing outside as we wait for the bell,
we have not seen our new classrooms yet.
New teachers, lessons, books, and friends,
and we know each class has its own **pet**!

We're having so much **fun** playing outside, and can't wait to see what's through that door.

We all went inside to our classrooms,
but there wasn't one pet to be found.
It seems they all watched us this morning,
and escaped for recess on the playground.

Now outside is crawling with class pets galore,
so in art class we drew traps to look at.

They figured out how to escape all at once,
who knew there was something called **Petchat**?

Lunchtime came, and we ran to the slide
to discuss who would catch which critter.
It looked like there were **NINE** on the loose,
not easy, but no one here is a quitter.

That's not a kid on those **monkey bars**!
From here it looks like a stick.
But sticks don't slither and wriggle around,
we better get over there quick.

Hiss...tory

So many kids are running and jumping,
then we see a **COMMOTION** on the slide.
Something is rolling down from the top...
Who knew that fur balls could speed glide?

Got to go faster, we're running out of time.
Check out the people playing four square.
That ball sure took a really high **bounce**.
Hold on, there are two things in mid-air!

There on the swings, just how is that moving?
There's nobody sitting on the top.
It's not really *windy* and don't think it's a ghost.
A hermit crab? How will she stop?

Still haven't found the rat, dragon, or spider,
but let's play! There's a rock wall to climb.
Wait just a minute, this part is so **sticky**.
We wonder, was he here this whole time?

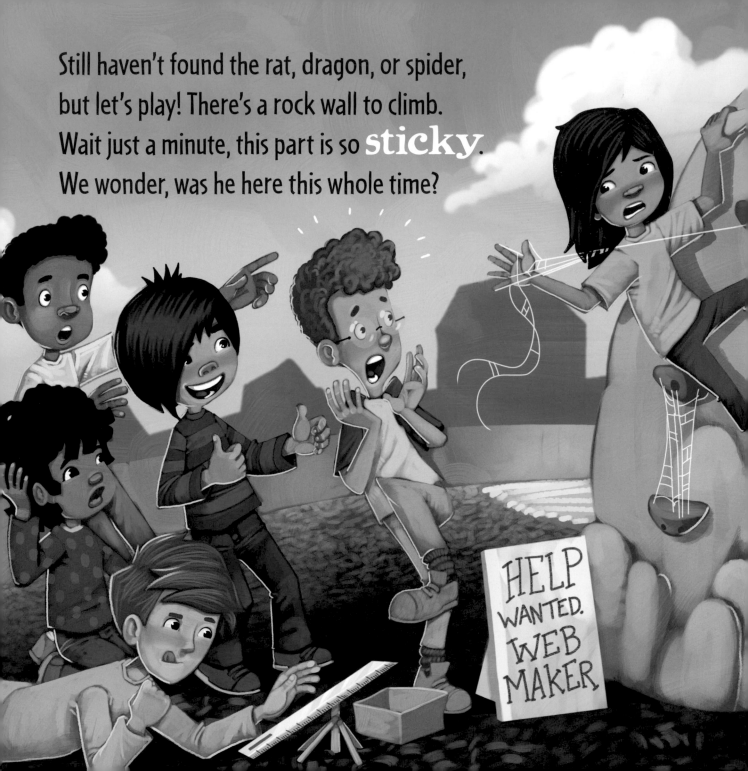

HELP
WANTED.
WEB
MAKER

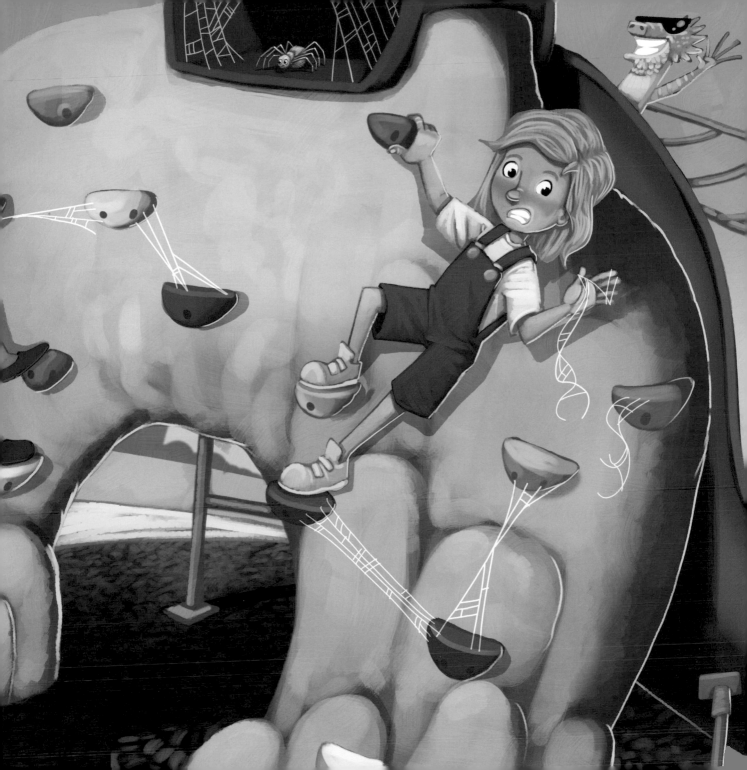

Teachers are calling, and lunch break is over.
Doesn't look like we caught any pets.
What was that? Did a rat leave the **tube**?
Maybe we just need better nets.

We never did find the **dragon**,
finding him might take us forever.
Well, at least the fish didn't get out.
You'd think they'd be bored but whatever.

Wow! How? The pets are all back!
Every kid let out a big **cheer**!
Can't wait for what happens tomorrow.
It's going to be a great year!

Recess ✓

Published by Sourcebooks Wonderland, an imprint of Sourcebooks Kids
P.O. Box 4410, Naperville, Illinois 60567–4410
(630) 961-3900
sourcebookskids.com

Cataloging-in-Publication Data is on file with the Library of Congress.

Source of Production: Wing King Tong Paper Products Co. Ltd., Shenzhen, Guangdong Province, China
Date of Production: December 2021
Run Number: 5024650

Printed and bound in China.
WKT 10 9 8 7 6 5 4 3 2 1